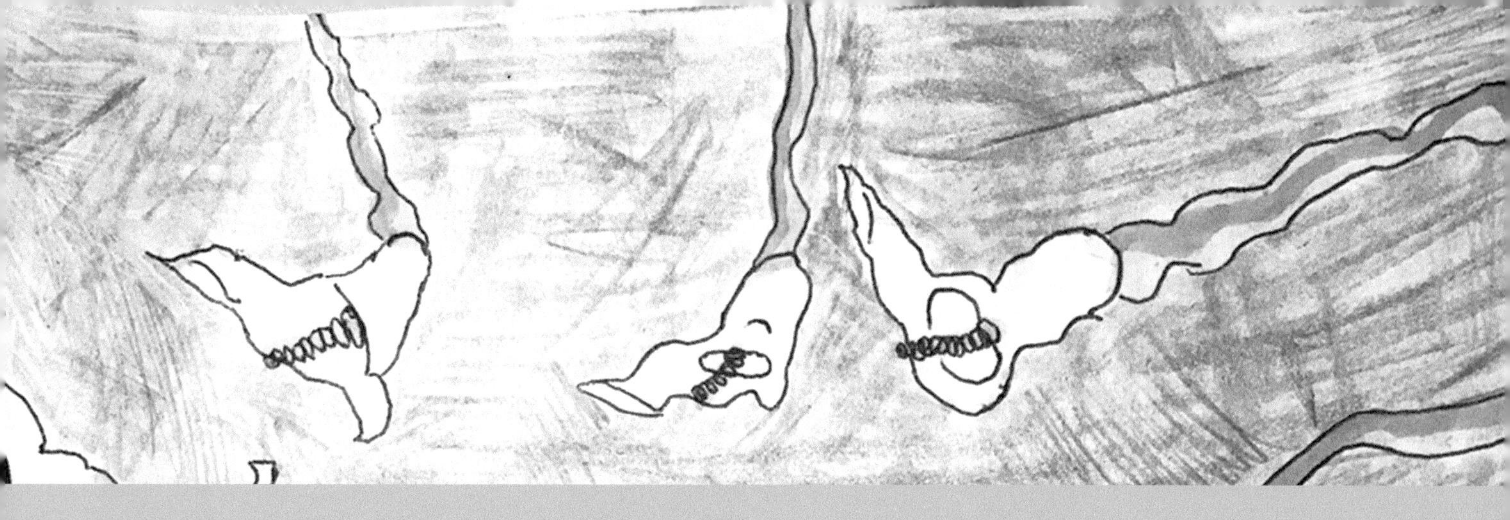

# Two Cows, the Snake and the Cubs

Michelle B. Davis-Brown &
Michelle A. Brown

Illustrations by Michelle B. Davis-Brown

AuthorHouse™
1663 Liberty Drive
Bloomington, IN 47403
www.authorhouse.com
Phone: 1 (800) 839-8640



Published by AuthorHouse 11/16/2016

ISBN: 978-1-5462-6925-0 (sc)
ISBN: 978-1-5462-6926-7 (e)

Print information available on the last page.



This book is printed on acid-free paper.



authorHOUSE®

Inspired by and dedicated to God.

Thank You to God in Christ.

Welcome to The Land of Zooilldephia. Here in

Zooilldephia all of the trees are ten feet tall.

So so tall, and yet the leaves

swing upon your face.

In Zooilldelphia there are two little Cubs.

Their names are Cub Kyle and Cub Susan.

The two Cubs were taken away from Mama Bear.

And so it goes, Cub Kyle and Cub Susan
had to live with the two big fat Cows.

The big fat Cows would not allow Mama Bear to see her Cubs.

So one day Mama Bear went

to the Zoo Keepers House of Adoption.

Hopefully, she would get to see her cubs

or have them back right away.

Once Mama Bear got to the

Zoo's House of Adoption,

she finally saw her Cubs.

Mama Bear ran over to hug one of her Cubs

but the Snake came along and

tried to pull away Cub Kyle.

Snake grabbed the little Cub's arm.

Oh no,?!....cried Mama Bear.

Then Officer Lion told Snake

to let the boy Cub go.

It was now time to be seen by the Chief Keeper.

Big fat Lady Cow and Snake were very close,

Snake laid on

fat Lady Cow's shoulder

during the time that the Cubs

were being talked about

at the Zookeepers House of Adoption.

Big fat Lady Cow and Snake spent a lot of time making up stories about Mama Bear.

This hurt Mama Bear and made her very angry,

so Mama Bear let out a loud roar!

Rooooooooar (in your best bear voice).

Lady Chief Keeper slams her

gavel and shouts order!

Sadly, she believed big fat Lady Cow

and Snake's made up stories.

So Lady Chief sided with the

big fat Cow and Snake.

Lady Chief wouldn't let Mama Bear have

her Cubs back.

This made Mama Bear sad, so she cried.

But this did not stop Mama Bear.

She wasn't an ordinary bear. She knew to pray.

It's her super power.

Mama Bear prayed to God in

heaven about her Cubs.

So Mama Bear prayed,

"Dear God, Please let me have

my two Cubs again."

Right away God spoke to Mama Bear.

She knew his voice,

God told Mama Bear He heard her cry.

Then God wiped the tears from her face.

God also told Mama Bear to

“Be patient and I will work it out”........

Meanwhile, at the hearing

Lady Chief Keeper told Mama Bear

she could see her Cubs

at least once a month.

Mama Bear smiled, she felt better.

God spoke again to Mama Bear,
“This is only for a little
time. Keep praying and soon you
will have your Cubs back.”
“Don’t forget, I will turn once a month
into a lifetime with your cubs.”

To be continued......

THE END,

for the cubs

The Two Cubs were taken away from Mama Bear in the land of Zooilldephia. Read to learn how through prayer and faith in God, Mama Bear is able to fight back and move closer to her dreams of being reunited to her Cubs. But this doesn't work out quite how she expected. In today's fast paced world, there are so many things teaching the opposite of how life really works. This book can be a good tool for generations to come wanting to learn how to patiently fight through trusting God in Christ through prayer.

.........in Jesus' name.

Printed in the United States
By Bookmasters